Pet Day

by Lucy Floyd
illustrated by Chris Lensch

Orlando   Boston   Dallas   Chicago   San Diego

Visit *The Learning Site!*

www.harcourtschool.com

It was Pet Day at
West End Park.

What a day! The
band played! Pets
ran! Pets sat in
laps and hats!

Jeb had a cat
with a bell. Peg
had her pet pig.

"What's Ed doing?"
Peg asked.

"The best pet
gets a ribbon!" Jeb
yelled. "We can't
miss that!"

"What pet gets
the ribbon, Ed?"
Peg asked.

"That is a surprise!"
said Ed.

8

"See the big red ribbon?" Ed said. "The best pet gets one like it!"

Peg held up her
pig. "Can a pig get
a ribbon?"

"Yes, a pig can get
a ribbon," Ed said.

Every pet
got a ribbon!